Officer's Report

Kayla Shields

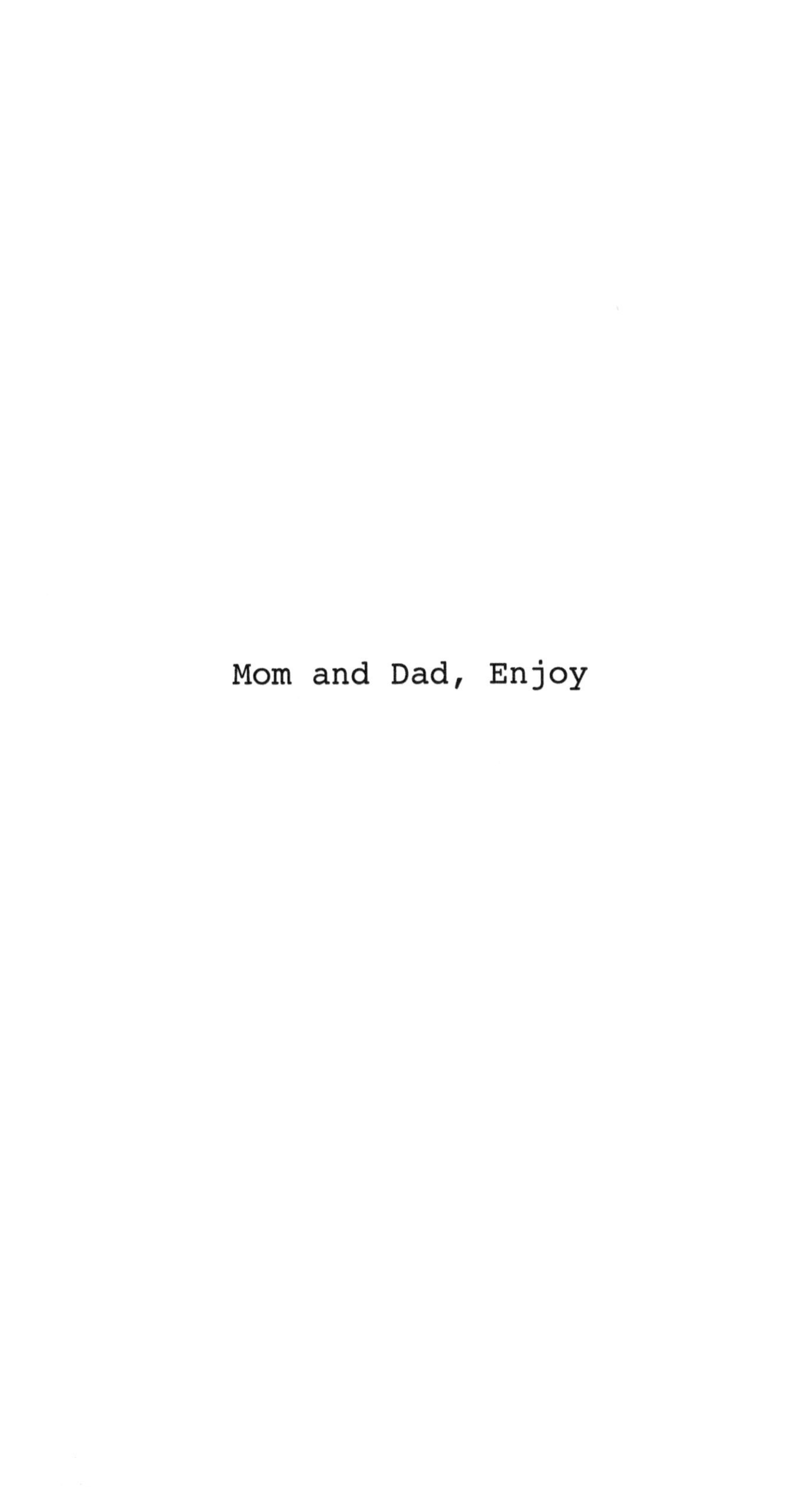

Mom and Dad, Enjoy

1

"This is officer Johnson requesting back up and the fire department!"

"What is the situation?" Dispatch asked.

"My partner heard a scream and ran inside. I was walking to the house when there was an explosion."

"Fire department is 15 minutes out. Backup is 10 minutes away."

I run back to the stairs for my partner. I search the top floor of the house for him. Once I find him, I throw his gigantic frame over my body. Once outside, I place him gently next to one victim.

"Kane, can you hear me?" I shout at Officer Taylor. I shake his shoulders.

"Sadie, I can hear you. You can stop shaking me," Taylor said, while gasping for air.

I watch the firefighters arrive and start running to us. I back away so they can help my partner.

"Anyone else inside?" one firefighter asked

"I am not sure. I found one victim in the first bedroom upstairs."

I watch them give officer Taylor air.

"Do you mind telling me what happened, Taylor?"

I heard a scream. I ran inside. I tried to get to the boy first.

"Kane," I say as I shake my head, "I didn't hear a boy scream."

He looks up at me from the grass. "What caused the explosion?"

"I don't know. I was right behind you. I thought I saw something out of the corner of my eye. I turned around, and you were gone."

"The fire is contained. It will take a while to see if you can go back inside."

"Did you find anything inside?" Taylor asked.

"No." The firefighter responded.

Taylor looks at me with a scrunched face. "How do we write this one?"

"I don't know yet. I am not convinced we only have one victim."

I look around. I take notes of the scene. The weather is a cool, crisp day. The sun is setting. I write about what is left of the house. The stairs are untouched. I write about the victim. One adult male. He seems to be early to mid 20s. I do a pat down. His pockets are empty. John Doe for now.

The hardest part of these cases is one simple question: was this is intentional?

As an experienced cop, I know witness are key to almost every new case we start. It doesn't seem like we have much to go on. I make a mental note to check records when we get back to the station.

I wait for Taylor to be checked out by the EMT.

Once he is cleared, we will ask the neighbors if they heard anything. We go door to door to find someone that saw something. It seems no one saw anything. We check one last house. "Did you happen to see anything suspicious about the time the fire broke out?"

"Yes, but I am not sure if I should say anything." The

witness responded.

"It is illegal to withhold information from law enforcement." I remind her.

"Alight. I will tell you, I saw someone running from the house just after you got there. I didn't know there was a fire or anything inside until the explosion happen. I heard a man scream."

I write down her statement as she speaks. I see the firefighters motioning for me.

"Taylor, take her information while I go talk to the Firefighters."

I walk back to Officer Johnson. "Our witness, Elizabeth, wants to see you," Officer Taylor says.

"I know who she is. Don't tell me you don't know her?" I asked.

"I am still new to this area. How am I supposed to know everyone?" Taylor snapped.

"She is on the city council." I said as I place my hands on my hips.

I watch the forensic team search the body. "There is gunpowder residue, but I do not see any wounds."

Alright. So it is safe to assume he was the one shooting not being shot at. With every passing moment, this case becomes more unusual.

I take a deep breath before walking over to Ms. Elizabeth's house.

"Elizabeth, do you mind coming down to the station with me?" I asked.

"I would, but I don't want to be involved. That is the most powerful family in the county." She looks scared. "Death always seems to follow that family," Elizabeth said as she crossed her arms.

"How do you know? Did you see the victim?"

"I am not sure who I saw, but in this neighborhood, you have to mind your business or they will come for you."

"Ms. Elizabeth, whose house is that?"

"Kyle McTeer's house," she whispered.

I look at her, even more confused.

I take a second to process what I've been told. Is it possible for the most powerful attorney to murder these people?

Now I have many questions to help me solve the crime.

1. What cause the death?
2. Could that be his son we found?
3. Is it possible to murder your own son?
4. How do we proceed with caution?
5. What cause him to snap?

Ms. Elizabeth, are you telling me everything you know? I look into her eyes. She looks scared. "It is ok, I can protect you but you have to tell me everything you saw or know."

I saw Kyle running up the stairs to get inside. That was strange. I heard gunshots, then I heard a female scream. I never saw him leave. Soon after the scream, I saw you and your partner run inside the building. I didn't see what caused the explosion.

Ok well considering your ties to the community, I do not deem it necessary to come to the station. I gave her my card in case she remembers anything else.

I nod, trying to process this information. "Did you tell Officer Taylor this?"

"Well, no, not exactly. I know he is new to the force. I didn't trust him with this information."

"Are you implying Kyle is responsible for this fire?"

Ms. Elizabeth looks terrified. "I cannot answer that."

I nod my head. "Please call me if you think of anything

else."

She takes my card from her hand.

"Sadie, please be careful.

"Always."

Our job here is done right now. We are going back to the station now. I watch Johnson get into my car.

"What did Ms. Elizabeth say to you?" Taylor asks.

"It is probably best you don't know."

Officer Taylor gives me a puzzling look.

"I've known Elizabeth my whole life. She and my mom were childhood best friends."

"I figured she knew you when she called you Sadie."

"Yes, it is rare to hear my first name while on the job."

We go back to the station. I wait for forensics to give me their analysis. I write my statement. I decide to leave Ms. Elizabeth's information out for now. I am lead on this case. I don't want officer Taylor or Elizabeth get hurt. I know what the McTeers are capable of.

"Are you leaving Officer Taylor?"

"Yes, unless you need anything."

"Actually, the scene should be clear now. I want to go back to see what else I can find."

He checks his phone. "Yeah, I will go with you."

"That is why you are my favorite partner."

I grab my keys and we walk to my car. I back out of the parking space when Taylor looks down at his phone.

"Is something wrong?"

"No, I was just thinking we could grab food on our way to the house?"

"Yeah, I am getting hungry too."

I drive to the closet fast food place. I order us two burgers and a soda. Watching Taylor down his food before I even finished with my fries.

"One day you are going to choke."

I finish my food, and we are almost back at the crime scene.

We arrive at the scene. I noticed the steps are the only thing left of the font. I look around the yard. Most evidence is lost or back at the station. I see one bullet shell on the ground in the sand. "You have any evidence bags in the car?" I yell to Officer Taylor.

"Yeah, I do." He brings me a few.

I bag and tag the shell. Carefully looking around the area, I still don't see anything else.

I start to walk to the house when we hear our names.

"Officer Johnson and Taylor, what are you doing back here?"

"Captain , I wanted to look at the crime scene more. What are you here?"

He looks down at his feet. "When I found out whose house this belonged to, I wanted to see it for myself. How are you doing, Taylor? I heard the firefighter pulled out."

"Actually, Officer Johnson pulled me and the victim out."

I can't believe this is actually his house. How does an attorney live on this side of town? I play back in my head how scared Elizabeth looked speaking to me. I carefully analyze her words to me. I don't understand what she meant by the most powerful family in the county. I've lived here all my life and never heard anything. I start to remember the amount of accidental deaths in this city. It has been a few months since we got the call about them.

I find the courage to ask the Captain   his opinions about this situation

"Hey Captain , do you think Kyle McTeer had anything to do with his house fire?"

"I think we all should proceed with caution."

I give him a puzzled look.

"One thing I have learned over the years, you do not get that much power and money by being so honest."

"Fair enough."

I hear officer Taylor attempting to speak.

"Do you think we should go inside the house?" Taylor's voice is shaking.

I look at the Captain . "Well, if you don't have any reason not to, I think it will be fine. We do have a job to do."

"No, no complaints, but I am going in with you."

I decide to take the lead.

I slowly open the front door again. It smells like burnt wood and paper.

Officer Taylor yells, "Watch your step."

I search the room downstairs. Unfortunately, there isn't much down stairs. I continue to walk up the steps. It doesn't look stable. I make to the first room on the left. I am beginning to feel anxious as this is the room I pulled Taylor out of.

"This looks like it was his office?" The Captain said.

"I don't see much of anything that can be saved from the fire. Taylor, can you check the desk?" My voice is shaking but also firm.

I decided to check the other rooms while they search the office. The room has the most black soot. I would say it started in here. I open the door slowly, unsure of what I am about to find. I would guess this is his bedroom.

"Officer Johnson! Johnson! Come back in here."

I rush back to McTeer's office. "Did you find something?"

"We aren't sure. It isn't labeled and has some damage."

"Alright, what is it?"

"A notebook with names in one column, another name in the next column, and payment in the next."

"He is an attorney. I am sure he does work at home, too. Bag it and I will look at it back at the station."

"It's dark. We should come back tomorrow when we have more time." The Captain said.

"I agree. The sun is almost gone, and we don't have enough flashlights."

We walk back to the cars in silence. I wish I knew more about Kyle McTeer. I hope tomorrow we will know the victim and more evidence. A case like this is going to be a high-profile case. I need to prepare Officer Taylor to speak to no one about this case. Especially considering who Kyle McTeer is. Interviewing his attorney's office will be the last thing we do if we can avoid it.

"Given who Kyle McTeer is and his connections to the community, we cannot speak about this investigation to anyone."

"I can do that."

I nod my head. I drop him off at the station. I decide to go home after work. I need a long, hot shower. I finally have to reflect on what Elizabeth said. How does death always follow this family? Who all is in the family? Tomorrow I will make a list of family members and hopefully see how death always follows that family, according to Elizabeth.

I walk into my small apartment. I take out my weapon and badge to place on my entry way table. I grab my favorite pajamas and head to the shower.

I get out of the shower, I still can not sleep.

I need to write all my thoughts about this case. I grab my notepad and pen. I grab my sticky notes to write major time lines. 3:46 pm phone call to 911. 4:00 We arrive. 4:14 house explodes from fire. 5:00 interviewing witnesses. Each time gets its own sticky note. Witness list is next. I write down Elizabeth's name. We have to find more witnesses. Now we have victims. One unknown male, and Kyle McTeer's home. I carefully go over my notes from Elizabeth. I still have nothing. I sigh in defeat. I try to look at it from a different angle. Could we connect Elizabeth to Kyle McTeer?

I have known her my whole life. What do I actually know about her? I start making a list.

1. Her name
2. She is on the city council since I was 10.
3. She never had a family.
4. She drives an expensive car
5. She lives in the wealthy area.

I do not know much about her life. She does seem to know a lot about mine. Does she have any relationship to McTeer? I start to think. My mind is tired. I glance over at the clock. It is midnight. I decide to put this away until tomorrow. I need sleep, so I can focus better tomorrow.

I walk to my bedroom and go to sleep.

2

I can't talk about the investigation with my mom, but I could call her about Elizabeth. I just need to leave out the details. I reach for my phone, dialing my mother's number.

"Hey Sadie," she answers.

"Hey mom, can I ask you questions about Elizabeth?"

"I guess."

"Has she ever spoke of Kyle McTeer?"

"That is her neighbor. They talk often, actually."

"Do you know if they had an argument?"

"No, why are you asking these questions, Sadie?"

"Well, Kyle's house was burnt down. I am just asking if they knew each other, ya know, off the record."

"Sadie." I can hear her sigh. "I don't think you should get close to this case."

"Why?"

"That family is not someone you want to cross."

"You are the second person that has said this and refuses to say why."

"Off the record, your dad was investigating a murder on the property when he was shot. McTeer's wife died and was found by their son Nathan."

"Do you think they had something to do with his death?"

"I don't know. Martin couldn't find anything."

"Captain Martin?"

"Yeah. There was no witness or evidence left at the scene."

"I have to go to work. I will call you later. And mom, don't mention this to Elizabeth."

"Alight, love you."

"Love you."

I hang up with my mother. I am surprised to find out this family may have a connection to my dad's murder. I wonder if Kyle McTeer has any idea who I am. I grab my things and head for the station. I have to tell Kane what I found out from my mother.

I run into the station searching for Taylor. He's sitting at his desk, looking busy.

"I called my mother and asked about Kyle and Elizabeth."

"Anything good?"

"Elizabeth and Kyle talk often according to my mom. We have to find proof of this."

"How?"

"Phone records, talk to other neighbors."

Kane checks his watch, "grab a coffee?"

I nod, "ill drive."

We rush through the station and into my car. I turn on the radio. I know I have to tell Taylor about my dad and his case. I turn the radio down before talking.

"My mother said they murdered my dad at the McTeer's lake house. There was no witness's or evidence. And Captain Martin eventually declared it a cold case."

"You think Elizabeth and McTeer know something about his murder?"

"It's not completely far fetched. My mother even said death follows that family but wouldn't get into it either."

"Isn't your mom and Elizabeth best friends?"

"Yes, but I have seen people kill for less. And with them both running for city counsel it's not that crazy to think."

"Well I see why you couldn't say that back at the station."

We arrive at the coffee shop, I order us 2 black coffee's. Taylor's head looks like it's about to explode from all this new information about my dad, Elizabeth and Kyle McTeer. My head is thumping from a headache forming. I search my cupholder for Tylenol to prevent it from getting worse.

We head back to the station. Taylor and I still have a lot to process for evidence. I get started on making case files. Since Kane and I have only worked together for six months, he is still learning. A high-profile case like this will grab media's attention pretty quickly. The longer it takes to solve, the longer we will have media surrounding this case. It's never my goal to rush any investigations, it is my goal to find the answers. Sometimes the answers are worse than not finding anything at all.

"Hey Taylor, want to go with me to look through the evidence found at my dad's crime scene?"

"Wouldn't it be all on the computer?"

"Possible. But I have to see the photos of everything."

We head down to evidence lock up. Luckily, we work at one of the smallest stations in the city. Everyone really helps each other here.

"Hey Johnson, what can I do for you?"

"I would like to see my dad's file."

"You sure?"

"Yeah." The officer lowers his brows at me. I know he is hesitant about giving me the file.

I watch the officer retrieve the file from the back. Taylor looks at me skeptically.

"Friendly gets you far with evidence lock up."

"I see that."

The officer comes back and hands me the file and McTeer's wife, Amanda, file.

"I'm not sure you will find anything useful in those. The files have been cold for a while. I thought you might want to see Mcteer's wife file too."

"You might be right."

I lay the file out on the table in the room, searching through photos of Amanda's file. I look through the evidence photos and crime scene photos.

"Pretty brutal."

Taylor's face scrunches looking at the crime scene. "There is so much blood. How could they not find a killer?"

"This is one of the most graphic ones I've seen."

I shift through my dad's. There really isn't much in there at all. I hand it back to the officer and tell him I will keep Amanda's file for a bit. We head back upstairs to look for a connection between the two cases. I need ballistics to give me something on the weapon that was found at McTeer's house. I start rubbing my face in frustration when I finally discovered something. It might not be relevant yet. Amanda was shot with a .22 rifle. We only found a 9mm at McTeer's house.

"Taylor, check to see what guns Kyle McTeer has registered."

"He has quite a few, actually."

"A .22 rifle or a 9mm?"

"Both."

"Amanda was shot with a rifle."

"Well, our victim wasn't shot, or if he was, we couldn't see it."

"They haven't given us an official autopsy yet."

"Call McTeer and ask him to come to the station."

I wait for Taylor to get off the phone. "He said he is busy, but can tomorrow come if we come to him?"

"Fine."

I could connect thinking about these two cases isn't as farfetched as I thought it would be. If only We could place the timelines, who was heard screaming and who shot. We do know the victim has gun shot residue on him. I need coffee, it really helps me focus.

The break room has coffee already made. I pour it into my cup, taking a sip as I process the new information. This should be an open and shut case and hopefully be able to close a cold case.

"Sadie, wanna grab dinner and call it a night?"

"Sure, I'll follow you to the diner."

We arrive at the diner. He finds us a spot at the counter. I order a salad and Diet Coke while he orders a steak and sweet tea.

"You have any plans this weekend?" Kane asked in between bites of his food.

"Samantha wants me to go to the beach this weekend. We shouldn't be working. You?"

"No, I need to clean my apartment."

"I should do that. Stitches is pretty messy," I said, joking.

Kane lets out a laugh. "I'm sure it is all stitches."

"Have you seen him eat? He loves to knock his food and water bowl over."

We finished our dinner. I decide to go home. Stitches is probably wanting his dinner by now. The traffic is horrible. It is tourist season. I wish I had more time to enjoy the beach and do tourist things on the weekend. I feel like I am always at my apartment with my cat.

I finally make it home and text Samantha, agreeing to go to the beach with her on Saturday. It is April so the water might be warm. Well, warm enough to cool us off after the sun overheats me. Stitches are curled up in my chair, sleeping. I pour his food into his bowl, which wakes him up. I leave him to eat while I get ready for bed.

15

3

I arrive at the station earlier than usual. I sit at my desk and begin to think about all the information I do have. This case is weird. I have so many questions not being answered. If I don't make progress within 48 hours, we lose more evidence and witnesses. I am stressed to the fullest.

We have to talk to Kyle McTeer today. I do find it suspicious he wasn't available to speak with us yesterday. I feel most people would be concerned about fire at their own house. Given Kyle's connection to the community, I am trying to have an open mind about this situation.

I watch Officer Taylor make his way to his desk. I stare at his face. He looks just as exhausted as I do this morning.

"I brought us coffee," Taylor said as he hand me a cup.

"Thank you, I needed this." I respond with a smile.

"Have a long night?"

"A little. I couldn't sleep. How are you feeling today?"

"Sore, my hip hurts from being thrown to the ground."

"You scared me. I was in a rush to get you to safety." I glance back at Taylor. "Next time, don't run into a building alone."

I sip on my coffee as I look at the time. It is only 7:30. Mornings always seem to go so slowly when I am waiting to do anything. I clean off my desk as I think about questions to ask Kyle McTeer today. My main question is, who was in your house? I actually have a lot of questions. I start writing them down so I do not forget. I hope we find more answers.

"We have to meet McTeer at his office at 9," Officer Taylor said.

I nod my head to him. I figured he would corporate today. Considering the circumstances, the Captain decided to let us question him today. I checked the hotel he was staying at. Everything seemed normal, according to the desk clerk.

"Why do lawyers start work at 9?" Officer Taylor asked.

"I really have no idea. I would imagine accommodating more clients." I glanced at Officer Taylor.

"Do you have a list of questions to ask, Kyle?" I nod to his computer.

"Yes, but I am sure you already thought of them."

"Perhaps, I have."

It is time to leave for McTeer's office. I grab my keys and head to the parking lot. Taylor is two steps behind me. We get into the car and I watch him rub his hands down his tighs.

"Nervous?"

"Aren't you? What if he confesses?"

"Then we arrest him and call it a day."

I give Taylor a smirk. "He will not confess if anything he will deny everything."

Searching for a parking spot, Taylor notices the cameras in the parking deck. I walk beside Taylor to Mcteer's office. We sit down waiting for him to come out.

"Hello Officers, follow me."

I follow behind Officer Taylor. I Place my hands on my hips as we walk into his office.

"I only have about 15 minutes before my client comes." Kyle said.

"We only have a few questions for you." Officer Taylor

says.

"Do you know the victim that was in your house?"

"No. I was at work all day. No one should be at my house."

"Can you think of anyone that might want to harm you, Mr. McTeer?" Officer Taylor asked.

"I am a member of this community. I am sure I have enemies, but I cannot think of anyone off the top of my head."

"Maybe a neighbor? Or a former client?" I suggested.

We watch Kyle shake his head.

Alright. This is going as well as I expected. Kyle is not willing to give us any helpful information. Something about this man irritates me.

"I have one question, officers." Kyle placed both hands on his hips.

We both nod.

"Do you have any suspects about the fire?" Kyle asked.

Officer Taylor looks at me. I smile back at him.

"At this time, no, but we are working to find some answers." I tell Kyle.

He escorts us out of his office. "I am staying at the hotel next to my firm, if you need anymore questions answered."

I watch Kane get into my car as I observe Kyle's office. I notice one security camera pointed to the door. I do not recall seeing any back doors in the building. I get in the car and drive to the backside. I was right, no other way out than the front door.

"Do you think we can get a warrant?" Kane asked.

"No, we don't even have probable cause at this point." I said.

"Something about that man just seems off."

"I found him absolutely irritating."

We just need to find anything that can tell us something.

This case becomes more irritating every second. I look at the clock. I am starving. I grab my snacks out onto the center console.

"I guess it is time to go ask Ms. Elizabeth if she can recall anything else," Kane suggests.

I let out a huff. "I would say so."

I start to drive to the other side of town when my phone starts ringing. I pull over to the side of the road so I can concentration on what I am being told. I pull out my notepad and pen as I start writing the information. I look over at Taylor, who is patiently waiting for me to relay the message.

"We have the name of our victim." I said.

Kane looks at me, waiting for the name.

"Damon Montgomery."

"Who is he in relation to Kyle McTeer?"

"I don't know. We are going back to the station to find out who he is."

"Yeah, that would be a good idea."

I drive quickly to the station. We both rush to our desk to find out about Damon. There has to be a connection.

I watch Officer Taylor start research on Damon Montgomery. I start to look for a possible motive. It seems like hours have passed and I still do not see a connection. Damon has a record of petty theft, but Kyle was never his attorney. They do not even live within a 20-mile radius of each other. I start to search the database for similar cases. There are several unsolved homicides in the city but nothing that is similar to our case. That does not seem like relevant information.

"How is the case going?" Captain asked.

"It is not going at all. We are back to the beginning."

I hear the Captain take a sharp breath. "Tread lightly."

"Are you thinking Kyle burned his own house down?" I asked the Captain .

"I do not know."

I bring out the drawing board. I recap what we know for sure now. There has to be a connection that we missed somewhere between the McTeer family and Damon Montgomery. I start to compile a suspect list. We have what could be two separate crimes: 1. Arson 2. Murder. For now, I think the same person did them.

"I have a theory." Officer Taylor said.

I look at him, "Ok what?"

"With the evidence we have, I believe Kyle walked in on Damon in his house and shot him and to make sure there is limited to no evidence, burned his house down," Taylor stated.

"I mean, it is possible, but why not call the cops? And You heard a scream."

"Think about it. We were called to the house for suspicious activity." Taylor said.

"I'm going to check with 911 to see who made the call."

I pace as I wait to see who made the 911 call and have the file sent to me. I hear the ping of my email. I sit in my chair as I listen to the audio. It is a man's voice. I hear the scream in the 911 call Officer Taylor said he heard. I only heard one gunshot on the audio. After I listen to the call. I see the neighbor's name that said he didn't see or hear anything.

"We need to bring Charles Line in for more questioning." I take a deep breath.

"Is that who made the 911 call?" Officer Taylor asked.

"Yeah." I said.

The suspect list now has three names on it. Elizabeth, Charles, and Kyle. This should be an easy close to the case. I just hope everything goes easily. I do not understand why Charles would lie about not seeing anything, but would call 911.

Officer Taylor drives us back to Charles' house for some

basic questions before we decide to interrogate him. Taylor starts to look nervous. I tried to explain that sometimes witnesses are not always reliable because information can change.

"I just don't know why he would lie to us." Taylor says.

"Sometimes witnesses do not want to be involved."

I let a long pause before I remind him to tread lightly in this case. We don't want to scare away any potential new information. I let Taylor take the lead on the questioning.

"Charles, we are here to see if you have any information about Kyle's house? Or if you heard anything?"

"I take it you heard the 911 call." Charles lets out a breath. "I am his neighbor. This side of my house has direct sight to his front door."

"Yes, I can see that."

"I didn't see anyone go inside the house except for Kyle. I heard a man scream, then gunshots. I think two, but I could be wrong."

I write down his statement. "Charles, did you see anyone burn the house?"

"No."

"In the call, you said there was suspicious activity. Can you explain what you saw?" Taylor asked.

"Yeah, Kyle was scanning the backyard. I thought this was odd because who checks the backyard before going inside? Then I heard the scream and called 911."

We think Charles for his time before we leave. Taylor and I agree that we can mark Charles off as a suspect. However, I cannot mark him as completely innocent since he wasn't so forthcoming during the initial questioning.

"Back to the drawing board?"

"No, I don't think so."

I watch Taylor send his phone to voice mail. "Want to get dinner after this?"

"I can't. I have to go see my sister after work." He tells me.

That is the worst part about being single. I eat alone most nights with my cat. I can't say I really mind, at least my cat understands I am a busy girl. I start thinking back on the night I rescued kitty. I was called to a scene I didn't see the suspect hiding behind a car. He ended up slicing my forearm with a knife, before my former partner arrested him. This small orange kitten came running up to me, rubbing against my leg. After I got out of the hospital, I went back to the scene looking for the kitten. He had no tags or id chip. The shelter said I had to wait 5 days before officially adopting him, so I did. The kitten is now a five-year-old cat named stitches.

"Sadie, where are you?" Taylor asked.

"Sorry, I was thinking about my cat and how I ended up with the cat." I replied.

"Oh. Interesting." Taylor nods.

We arrive back at the station, I decide to go home. There isn't much we can do today.

Once I arrive home, stitches is patiently waiting on me by the front door. "I know, you are hungry too." I feel him brushing against my legs. I start to tell kitty about my day and the case. Sometimes it helps me to talk about it out loud to make connections together.

I start to put sticky notes on my wall with possible theories and connection. Other than being neighbors, they don't seem to have much in common with all three of them. I don't know much about Charles, but tomorrow I will look into him. There is something we are missing.

I decide to take a break and watch TV before bed with stitches. He loves to curl in my lap as I watch TV. I start to fall asleep when stitches jumps off my lap. He starts to walk to my bed and I follow.

4

My phone ringing wakes me up. My alarm hasn't even gone off yet.

"Yeah?"

"Sounds like I woke you up. I need you at the station like now."

"What is wrong, Kane?"

"I got here early. Another witness came forward. He wants to be anonymous. "

"Ok, well, who is it?"

"Anonymous means I don't know Sadie. Be at the station at 6:45."

I hang up the phone. I glance at the time. I have just enough time to make a cup of coffee and get dressed. I rub my face, trying to wake up. I slowly make my way to the kitchen before I get dressed to start the coffeemaker. I rush to get myself ready for the day. Grab my badge and weapon. I pour my coffee in my tumbler and went off to the station. I drink my coffee pretty fast on the drive there. I am desperately trying to wake up still.

I pull into the parking lot. I see Officer Taylor outside, waiting for me. I nod to him. "So, why are you here so early?"

"Something about this case doesn't make sense."

I can't disagree. Everything about this case doesn't make sense at all. Why is a witness coming in after the fact when we already asked all the neighbors? Unless it is not a neighbor.

We walk into the station. I sit at my desk, waiting for our visitor. 6:45 passed and still no one. I look over at my partner, "Are you sure it was AM and not PM?"

He looks at his desk. "He didn't say, he just said 6:45."

To pass time, I will find more information about Elizabeth and Kyle's connection, if they even have one.

I pull up her house information. She bought it in 2012 for 1.2 million. That is an insane price for a home, even if it is in the historical district. Thankfully, this is all public knowledge, so if she was hiding something, she wouldn't have bought such an expensive house. I wonder how much city council pays for her to be able to afford her life style. I had to do some more digging. She makes 50,000 yearly. Now red flags are starting to rise. How does one make 50,000 have a 1.2 million dollar home and a 105,000 dollar car? That makes no sense. I am not seeing any connection to Kyle McTeer yet.

It is a far stretch, but maybe she is working with McTeer off the record. Could I even make the connection? I need to research Kyle McTeer.

A shadow cast over me. I look up slowly. It is Kyle McTeer himself.

"How can I help you?"

"I am the one that called this morning. I have information to discuss with the officers on my case."

"I see. What can you tell me?"

"I was coming home from work when I was seeing the fire. I called 911. I think I know who started the fire."

"Who do you think did it?"

"My neighbor, Elizabeth Flower."

I write down the information he gives me. "Why do you think she would do it?"

"Because she knew I was running for city council. She thinks I am going to take her job."

"So she burned your house down?"

"Yes."

"Why couldn't you tell us this at your office?"

"I don't completely trust the people in the office. You never know who she might be working with."

"Then why keep them?"

"Good workers are hard to find."

I arch my eyebrows and continue to write the information down.

I think Kyle is paranoid now. Who in their right mind would suspect a neighbor just because they are both running for office? Not only that, but who keeps employees when you can't trust them? That sounds suspicious and paranoid.

I have more questions about this now. According to McTeer, I have a motive for Elizabeth. It still doesn't make sense why she would be a witness to a crime she committed unless she wants to throw us off. Then it doesn't make since why Charles was the one that made the 911 call.

He observes my desk. I will wait until he leaves to write notes about connections.

"I hope to hear from you soon, Officer Johnson."

I nod.

"That was not who I was expecting." Officer Taylor responded.

"Me either, and I wasn't expecting him to say he thinks Elizabeth did it."

"What are your thoughts, Taylor?"

"My gut is telling me Kyle McTeer isn't innocent."

"Yeah, I get that feeling, too."

"So what do we do?"

I wish I knew the answer to that. I know we need to interview Elizabeth again. We still don't have motive, means, or opportunity figured out. I doubt Kyle McTeer is even telling the truth.

"Well, let's go visit Elizabeth again."

I let Officer Taylor drive. Once we get there, I think of questions to ask her. Maybe we should make her sweat and tell her what our source told us. This is a bad plan, but here goes nothing.

We slowly walk up to the door.

"We have more questions for you."

"Come in."

We walk to her table. I take a deep breath.

"What question do you have now?"

"Our source told us they believe you have responsibility for the fire."

"Oh! That is absurd. I would never do anything like that."

"What is your relationship with Kyle McTeer?"

"He is my neighbor. He wants to run for city council president."

Officer Taylor raises his eyebrow.

"Do you have any conflict with him?"

"Goodness, no I don't."

I raise to stand. "Thank you for your time."

We walk back to the police car. I need more time to process this situation. Taylor keeps asking too many questions. He isn't even asking the right questions.

"Do you think Elizebeth is embezzling?"

"At this point, I think neither one is innocent. But the crime we have, I don't know if either is innocent at this point. I think they are guilty of separate crimes."

We leave Elizabeth's house for the station.

"We need to look into Charles."

"I will do that right when we get there."

I start to look up any weapon Elizabeth may own. My search keeps coming up with nothing.

"Elizabeth doesn't own any weapons. Find anything on Charles?"

"Nothing. Not even a speeding ticket. I did find he inherited his house. His parents owned the marina."

"Does Charles own it?"

"No, he sold it to the city after his parents died in 2008."

"Safe to say Charles is not a suspect. Just called 911."

I would like to think Elizabeth is innocent and was not the person screaming in the 911 call. Everyone said it sounded like a man except Elizabeth. A witness isn't always reliable. Only two suspects. This isn't looking good and also isn't looking like an open and shut case after all. I can't call my mom again. I shouldn't have even called her in the first place. Answers will start to surface once the evidence is processed and hopefully that is soon.

5

"Johnson, you have mail."

"Can you put it on my desk?"

I finish pouring my coffee. I open the package left on my desk. A 9mm. I drop the weapon and flip the package over to see who sent it.

"Anyone know who sent this package? Was it delivered or in the mail?"

"It was left on the steps this morning."

Taylor's face is frozen in shock.

"Is that the murder weapon?" Taylor asked.

"I doubt we will get that lucky, but I am going to send it down to see if it matches the bullet we found at McTeer's house."

"I will go with you."

If this matches the bullet found at the house, this could be the first actual piece of evidence to connect Kyle to the murder and arson. I am still waiting for the fire department to identify the accelerant. I should call them to see if they found anything that maybe we missed or they forgot to call. The lack of evidence, I am becoming less hopeful this will be solved anytime soon. I need witnesses or more evidence. Even then, we get a chance to interrogate Kyle. We get 90 minutes. I know he will lawyer up real quick. He will not talk once he gets a lawyer and knows we find him to be a suspect. I need to keep him from learning he is a suspect.

"Taylor, did you find any feet prints at the scene?"

"No, considering I was on oxygen, I think Officer Bryce was looking."

"I will check again with him."

We have several tire prints, one set being mine, one set being Kyle's and one partial, which we do know is used by trucks. Since it is at Kyle's house, it is not really evidence. I need this weapon to match and have someone's fingerprints on it. Who ever delivered this to me, must also want to see Kyle blamed or know something.

"We need to dust the package to see if there are any fingerprints. Maybe that will lead us to something."

"At this point, I will take anything."

I grab the dust kit, starting to brush the dust looking for any signs of prints.

"I found a partial. Can you see if it is in the system?" I asked Taylor.

"Yeah, let me get tape."

Taylor is scanning the partial finger print hoping to get some hint of whose it might be. This could take a while, since it is only a partial print. Taylor turns to face me. His face is tense.

"Who do you think sent it?"

"It could be a number of people, Kyle, Elizabeth, anyone that knows we are looking into them. It could be a distraction to lead us away from Kyle or Elizabeth."

Taylor turns back to the computer. I look to see what it says. The computer is still searching through the database.

I grab the weapon and start searching for fingerprints on it. I grab two prints from it. Next, I will check for blood. Taylor's eyes light up like Christmas lights when the barrel of the gun starts glowing. We need to take this to forensics, like now.

Taylor grabs me an evidence bag. We pace to the elevator. I hit the first floor and the ride down is silent. The doors open and we are greeted.

"I need this tested for the bullet we found at the house and to find out whose blood this is. And as fast as possible, please," I said while handing it over.

"Where did you find this?"

"It was delivered to the station left on the steps addressed to me. I am not totally hopeful it is for our case, but we might get lucky."

"Rush job it is."

I smile at the forensics scientist and turn to leave. I have to tell the Captain about the box being delivered. Maybe the camera or someone saw who left it. We rush up to his office.

I knock, waiting to be addressed.

"Johnson, come in."

I stand behind the chair in front of his desk.

"I heard about the package, do you have any updates?"

"We found a partial finger print on the box, two finger prints on the gun and blood on the barrel."

"I don't like how easy this was. I want you to go home for the day. I will call you if we get results form the test."

"Respectfully, no. I want to be here. Plus this place is a lot safer than my apartment if I am a target."

Captain lets out a sigh, "If you wish but I think you should think about going home. I really don't like this."

I turn on my toes to leave his office. I can't believe he tried to send me home for receiving it. I highly doubt I am the target, I fully believe someone knows something and wants to truth out.

Since there is nothing left for me to do here, I think I am going to go home. I could use a day of rest.

6

The suspense about the weapon is literally making me impatient. I decided to go home and check on stitches. I am sure forensics will call if it is important.

I get home and curl with stitches. Beginning to brainstorm about this case, I think I might find a breakthrough. It's only been a few days. We still haven't got anywhere with suspects or witnesses. My Captain insists on not going undercover. I also firmly believe it is better to ask for forgiveness than ask for permission.

I start to think as it pet stitches in my lap. I need to work on the timelines. Connect the dots between the Kyle, Damon and Elizabeth. I start to wonder if I can even connect Elizabeth to the crimes. How she is so successful? Is it possible she actually worked her way to the top of the ladder? I would think almost anything is possible. I need to focus on the facts of this case, not the what ifs. Elizabeth is not a suspect right now.

What I do know is that Kane Taylor is being weird lately. Every time his phone rings or even a text, he seems to be hiding his phone. Even if it is all in my head, I don't want to ask the one person I depend on if he is hiding something. That is, being a terrible partner.

Maybe paranoia is getting the best of me. I take several deep breaths as I try to calm down. Perhaps I will never know the truth unless I go undercover, which the Captain has already told me was a no. Since I couldn't convince him, maybe Taylor can.

I stand to pace around my small apartment. I rub my face with my hands. I need a shower and a clear head. The thoughts are heavy about how I still don't have any answers. I can't close a case without them. I would like to keep my 89 percent conviction rate. I get out of the shower, while deciding tomorrow is a new day. A new day with more answers waiting for the right questions to be answered. I curl up with my kitty. I feel like I tossed and turned all night long.

I wake up with the sun shining into my bedroom. My kitty paws at my face. I stretch as I reach for my phone to check the time. I wake up before my alarm goes off. I get dressed. I decided since I am up so early I will go get coffee instead of making it at home. I grab my gun and my badge as I run out of the door. I rush down the stairs outside leading down to my car, hopefully making it without having someone call telling me they need me at the station.

I grab coffee for Taylor and me. If I need to observe him, I need to see who is calling him. Maybe I am over thinking about Taylor. He is pretty new to the department. I start scheming about it on my way to the station. I want to know more about Taylor's past. I know he was a troubled kid, but I do believe in second chances. That is the whole principal of juvenile justice, or even the whole justice system. That rehabilitation is possible. I also believe it really is never an open/shut case.

I walk to Taylor's desk.

"I woke up early, so I got us both coffee."

"Thanks, I had a rough night." He smiles back at me.

I nod my head in observance. He has a rough night also, that seems interesting. How can someone whom lives alone have such a long night? I think about the question; I live alone and most nights they do seem long.

I start to think of people I can ask questions about Taylor too, but I quickly realize I never see him with anyone other than me. Even working with him every day, I don't know anything. I will make time to get to know him after working hours. I sit down at my desk; I check my emails. I don't have any updates on my email or phone calls.

I hear Taylor's phone ringing behind me. I turn to look his way. He nod his head to me as he walks away from his desk. I was half tempted to follow him, but it looked like a personal call. I shake it off. It is probably his sister calling. I step out to find Kane. Despite how I may feel at the moment, I do care about him. I picked him to be my partner. I knew he was a great cop and would be a great detective. Lately, he is just acting weird.

"You alright?" I said as I placed my hands on my hips.

"Yeah, it was my sister. She is worried about me being in this case."

I scrunch my face together. "You mean she is scared of Kyle McTeer?"

"She dated one of his sons."

"I went to high school and college with one of his sons. He was a nice boy, very quiet and stay away from everyone." I crossed my arms. "I was actually friends with him in college. He was in a few of my classes. We would study together, but he never spoke about his family." I said as I rubbed my hand over my forehead.

"Could you ask him about this case? Maybe see where he was at?" Taylor asked.

"I can try. We haven't really talked since

college."

I go back to my desk; I send Nathan, McTeer's oldest son, a quick email to catch up. I hope he does email me back. We lost touch after college.

"I sent Nathan an email."

Taylor nods his head towards me.

"Can you talk to the other son?" I asked Taylor.

"I don't know about it being a friendly talk, but I can as a detective."

"Let me talk to Nathan first, then we will decide if the other brother is needed."

"What happened between your sister and McTeer's son?"

"She was dating him when his mother died. He didn't take it well. He thought his dad had something to do with it. My sister ended things not too longer after that."

I am still waiting for everything to be processed in this case, so we do not have much to do today. Taylor also hasn't heard anything back from anyone either. It is finally lunchtime, so I take Taylor to go get food with me.

I hear my phone ding.

"Nathan finally emailed me back!"

Taylor looks at me closer. "Well?"

"We are meeting at the coffee shop tomorrow."

I roll my eyes when I read the time. I wanted to sleep in on Saturday. Who goes to a coffee shop at 7 in the morning? I let out a huff before I email Nathan back, only because I think it would also be nice to catch up with him. I have to set my focus back on work.

"Do you think we should follow McTeer yet?" Taylor said as he turned towards me.

"I don't think the Captain will allow it."

I study his face for a moment. He seems like he is hiding something.

I watch as Taylor's phone rings, he pulls it out of his pocket and hits ignore. His lips form a straight line.

"Everything alright?" I say.

He nods back at me.

"If you need to talk, I'm here."

I should focus on waiting to hear about the weapon. Last time I checked, forensics was back up and trying to catch up. I should have told them about a rush job with an emphasis on rush. Clearly, they are overworked.

I don't understand why Kane is being so weird about taking phone calls unless he knows more about this case and Kyle McTeer than he is leading me to believe. I work up the questions to ask him, so he doesn't think I am up to anything.

"Do you personally know McTeer?" I asked Kane.

"No, I have just seen him around town."

"Why did he look at you like that when we went to his office?"

"Maybe he thought he knew me from somewhere or my sister," Taylor said.

I place my hands on my hips. "I was just trying to figure out why you are acting weird lately."

"I have a bad feeling about this. I think my sister is scared because she also believes Kyle killed his wife. I also know their housekeeper is missing and has been for years."

"Wait what? A housekeeper?"

"It is just what my sister told me."

Against better judgment, I am going to follow Kane tonight. I don't believe him at all. What Taylor said about the other brother makes me question why he can't speak to him. Kane has to know more than what he is telling me. I don't understand why he feels like he can't trust me with this.

7

I watch Taylor leave the office. I quickly finish what I am doing, so I can get snacks and stuff for tonight. I wish I had someone to call to keep me company. My only friend, Sam, is actually a lawyer and would never agree to this. I can't blame her at all.

I get into my car and drive to get coffee first. I have to wait until I get all the essentials. I am making good timing. I got everything I need in less than an hour. I make my way to Taylor's apartment. While searching for a place to park, I make sure I am not too far from him. I need to see if he leaves or if anyone comes to him. Kyle McTeer would never be the type to show up at Taylor's apartment if something was going on.

I pull out my phone to waste some time. Sam called to see if I wanted to go get dinner tonight. I hate lying to her, but she can't know. I see someone leaving Taylor's apartment. I Can't see since it is dark. My eyes follow the person to Kane's car. Now is my time to get answers.

I slowly follow behind Kane's car so he doesn't notice my car. Since it is dark, it shouldn't be hard to stay unnoticed. I feel like we have been driving forever. It seems like we are not stopping anytime soon. I fall back when we get closer to a shipping yard.

I grab my binoculars. I see him walking into a building. I am in disbelief that he is meeting with Kyle McTeer. I can hear my heavy breathing. I know I need to get closer to hear what is being said. Why is my partner meeting with Kyle McTeer, of all people? Kyle isn't a good person. We both believed he killed his wife. I can't believe what I am seeing.

I take a deep breath to clear my thoughts. I need to get closer. I quietly get out of my car and sneak to the side of the building. As I walk to get closer, I notice a window. I can't believe I am going to do this. I run to the side of the building and crawl to the window. I get as close as possible without being noticed.

I peek into the window so I can verify it is Kyle and Taylor in the building. I gasp when I see I am correct. I suddenly realized I do not have my service weapon on me. I check my pockets. I can not get caught. I don't have anything on me.

I calm myself down. I try to listen to what is said. It is too quiet. I can't hear anything said. I know I can't go inside or I will be noticed. I watched their body language. Taylor starts to back away and crosses his arms. He seems like he doesn't want to be there.

I notice Kyle with his hands on his hips. His face looks concerned. I take a mental note of what he is wearing. All I can see is a polo shirt. I wish I could hear what he was saying to Taylor. I try to press closer to the glass on the window. Still can't hear anything. I convince myself to not rush in and save my partner. He came here on his own. I don't know if I should even ask Taylor about this. I don't want to be accused of not trusting my partner. He is the one person that is supposed to have my back on this job. If I am wrong, this could jeopardize my career or his.

The thunder is rumbling in the distance. I pull out my phone and a storm is coming from the ocean to shore. I snap a photo and get out of there before they realize I am here. I quietly make my way through the dark back to my car. The storm is moving quick. I grab my phone to check the photo. If I am going to confront Kane about this, I need a clear photo.

The drive back to my apartment, my mind is going crazy. I turn up the radio to drown out the noise in my mind. The rain starts pouring down on my window. I am suddenly happy I decided to leave. How can I even trust my partner anymore? I try to reason with myself that Kane is innocent until proven guilty. He looks so suspicious tonight with Kyle McTeer. What kind of relationship could they even have?

I need to poke a round more. I finally make it home and walk up to my apartment. Stitches is waiting for his dinner. He pushes against my leg. I reach down to give him a scratch behind his ears. I fill his bowl before I threw my badge on the table. I take a deep breath and sit in my chair. I feel the tension leave my shoulder as I lean back.

I rub my forehead with my left hand. I hear a knock at my door. I check the time. It is pretty late. Who would be here at this time?

I open the door. To my surprise; it is Kane Taylor.

"We need to talk now."

I open the door to let him in. "All right, come in."

"Sadie, I know you were following me tonight." I hear him sigh. "Please do not get involved with this."

I place my hands on my hips. "Kane, what is going on?" I rub my forehead again. "Do you know how guilty you look right now?"

"I can explain, but you have to trust me."

"You're asking for a lot. So you better start talking now."

I observe Kane moving to my couch. Stitches come running to him. I move closer to him.

"Kyle wanted to meet with me to find out what you know about him."

"And what did you tell him?"

"I told him we didn't know anything about the murders and we do not have ballistics back from the bullet we pulled from the body."

"Did he admit to the crimes or just poke around without trying to raise attention to anyone?"

"Sadie, I think he is looking pretty guilty right now."

I sit in my chair across from Kane.

"I have a feeling this is bigger than we both know."

"If he is willing to ask a cop, then he definitely knows more than what he is saying."

I process that conversation. I sigh a little louder than I should out of frustration. I literally don't know what to say. I look up and notice Kane is still staring at me.

"Are you ok?" Kane asked.

"I am more confused, but I am ok."

"I just didn't want you to think I had something to do with the murders."

"I didn't think you were involved. I just knew you were acting weird. You should have come to me as a friend."

"I know, but I don't want you involved with his plan. He wants me to try to sabotage the investigation."

"We have to take his to the Captain . We may have enough for warrants or at least a be able to follow and go undercover."

"Sadie, this is dangerous."

"It's a part of the job."

Taylor stands up to leave. "Sadie, be careful tonight."

I lock the door behind him. I am glad he came to me after the fact, but I wish he would have before. I could have given him a wire and had more evidence Kyle was trying to manipulate the investigation. At least we know we are getting closer to finding out the truth. Kyle is getting worried, which means he knows more than what he said. We have to look at this from Kyle being guilty versus Kyle and Elizabeth working together.

We will question Kyle again. I will find answers I need to close this case.

8

I want to believe in my partner. I just can't seem to justify his choices of meeting with McTeer. I fear I need to get the Captain involved, but how would that look if Kane is innocent? We all have monsters from our past trying to bring us down. Luckily for me, my monster is different. I don't want to end up like my dad and die while on duty. I swallow back the pit in my throat, wondering what I need to do.

Stitches curling up in my lap. Meowing that it is time to eat, but I can't help but ignore his meows while I think about tonight. I slowly walk to get stitches some food, then maybe I can think more about the situations before me.

I toss and turn all night, wondering what the Captain would say about this.

My alarm is extra loud this morning. I feel like I didn't even go to sleep. I take a quick shower before making coffee. The drive isn't as bad since the tourist aren't usually awake at this time for the morning.

I arrive at the station wondering why no one is here this morning. I glance at the clock. 4:30. That explains a lot. Night shift is still on duty. I park my car in my usual spot and grab my coffee. I go straight for my desk to research Kane Taylor. Obviously, he can't have a record since he is a cop. I start

41

digging and I can't find anything in the system. I go to social media to see if his profiles are public. Of course they aren't. He is good at hiding his personal life, which is good in this line of work. Most people that commit homicide aren't good people.

"You're here early, Johnson."

"Yeah, I actually wanted to meet with you in private."

I follow closely behind the Captain . I shut the door behind me.

"My partner, Taylor, met with McTeer last night."

"Ok."

"I think he's working with him to cover some crimes."

"What do you want to do?"

"I want to stake out McTeer and see if Taylor comes back."

"Sadie, you're a good cop, but I don't think this would be a good idea."

"Why?"

"Do you know how powerful this man is? He is a legacy. His family has held that power for a reason."

"I know, but with Taylor's help, we might actually get something."

"No."

I pace around.

"Sadie, sit down."

I listen and sit down, Captain 's face turn serious. His eyes are wide and his lips are straight line.

"The blood that was found on the gun, is your dads."

"The finger prints did not come back with a match, neither did the set on the package."

I pivot on my toes and walk out of his office. How can this man defend McTeer. He committed murder, burned down his own house and there is nothing we can prove. Someone delivered me the weapon that was used to murdered my dad, while at McTeer's house. I have to get more information out of Taylor.

Why does not one single person believe he is capable for murder or arson? This family is surrounded by death and no one blinks an eye.

I spot Taylor rounding the corner. I let out a breath I didn't know I was holding.

"Hey," Taylor says while passing my desk.

"Hi."

The tension is thick.

"I'm sorry I scared you last night."

"You are the one person that is supposed to have my back while our life is on the line. Not meet sketchy people behind my back. You could have been killed."

His stare is glaring me down. I can't tell if he is amused or actually understanding I care for him as a person.

I stare at my computer, getting ready to write a case report. Although there isn't much to write since we still do not have anything.

"I'm going back to forensics to see if they have anything else?"

"Yup, I am behind you."

We walk in silence to the elevator. The doors open, I walk in first pressing the 4th floor. Taylor comes and waits on the other side. He hits the emery shut off.

"Sadie, please forgive me. I don't like you being mad at me. I am just trying to protect you."

"From what?"

"Kyle McTeer."

I take a hard swallow. Rubbing my hands over my face.

"What do you mean?"

"I'm worried if you get too close, you might be next."

"Did he say that?"

"Not in those words, but he did say that he wants to point the cops in a different direction. And since I am the cop on the case, he offered me money."

"Where is the money and how much?"

"In my car, I don't know what to do with it. And half a million."

I let out a sigh. "Just hold it. It might be evidence later."

"The weapon that was delivered has my dad's blood on it. He was murdered at McTeer's house investigating his wife's murder."

"Oh Sadie. I don't even know what to say. Do you want to talk about it?"

"No."

I start the elevator again.

"What does this family have on you?"

"I used to steal cars for them so they could run drugs down the coast."

Well, this case just got entirely more complicated. While I don't like it, I atlas have a plan I can work with now. I just hope Taylor and the Captain are up for a crazy plan.

We walk into forensics together.

"Hey guys."

"Got anything yet?"

"Nothin', well, there is nothing else to give so far. I assume you know about the blood on the weapon?"

"Yep."

"Do you think Elizabeth is willing to tell us anything more?" Taylor asked.

"I doubt it. She made it clear she does not want to be involved."

"I didn't eat breakfast. Wanna grab some and we can go at least drive by her house."

I nod in agreement. I think Elizabeth would be a dead end, since she was very adamant about not being involved.

I let Taylor drive, since I still have my coffee.

"Ya know, this fast food is terrible for you." I glare my stare hard at Kane.

He rolls his eyes at me and continues to order.

Elizabeth's home isn't too far from here, so we swing by. It's still dark outside and still dark inside her home. I get out of the car and walk around the perimeter of the house. Her car isn't even here. I supposed she is at work. I get back into the car and feel an eerie feeling as we drive past McTeers' house. It's even more creepy now that it's starting to cave in on itself.

"Sadie, can you do me a favor?"

Hesitant, I open my mouth, "depends on what it is."

"Can I stay on your couch tonight?"

"Don't even tell me why and yeah."

Something is telling me to trust him, but with his actions, it's becoming harder. I exhale as we pull back up to the station. Something about his driving makes me so car sick. I know he likes to drive the car.

Today was wasted and I guess the both of us could try to convince the Captain to let us go undercover. I doubt he will even agree to that.

"Hey think if we both ask the Captain to go undercover he will let us?" Taylor asked like he was reading my mind.

"Not a chance. He keeps denying me."

We slowly walking to the building. I sit down at my desk while Taylor stands next to me.

"Johnson and Taylor, my office now!"

Kane glances at me. I shrug my shoulders, wondering what we did now. I follow behind Kane's tall stature. I shut the door behind me as Kane is already sitting down.

"Did you go back to Elizabeth's home?"

We exchange glances. "I did a search of the property. I thought she could be more helpful."

"She called complaining that two officers entered her home and destroyed it."

Kane's eyes lock on mine.

"We did not enter the home. While we were there, the lights were off and her car was gone." I said.

"What time did she report this?" Taylor asked.

"She called about 10 minutes ago."

"We were already back at our desk by then." I stated.

I can tell the Captain is growing impatient with us.

"Go check it out."

I tell Kane to meet me at the car. I have to grab the keys off of my desk. I walk as fast as I can. Who in the department would even think to go see Elizabeth? They wouldn't even think of going.

I drive as fast as possible to Elizabeth's home. On the way, I call my mom to see if she is with her. Kane is side eyeing me the whole time.

"You really think your mom wouldn't call you if your only witness showed up at her house?"

"I haven't told my mom about this case."

We arrive at Elizabeth's house. Still dark and still no car. Something doesn't feel right about this. I walk up the steps to the front door while Taylor takes the back door. I peer into the windows. Everything is scattered on the floors and across the tables. I check to see if it is locked, and to my surprise; it is not locked. I radio Taylor, saying to enter.

I observe the mess, looking for any clues to what happened.

"It looks like a struggle back here," Taylor yells.

I place my hand on my gun and finish walking to the kitchen. I see a note on the table address to me.

1.8 Million dollars. Wired by 8pm or she dies.

Kane walks up behind and reads the note. "Well, well."

"It wasn't cops that entered her home, nor was it her who called."

I call the Captain to tell him what we found. He is sending

more uni's to us.

"Kane, if you know anything at all, you have to tell me."

"I don't." He shakes his head in disbelief.

"Is this why you wanted to stay on my couch?"

"Well, I was afraid they had my place staked out. And now I bet they have yours, too."

This day just keeps getting worse. I call my mom back to warn her to lock the doors and do not let anyone inside, even if they say they are cops. I can hear the fear in her voice.

"Mom, is dad there?"

"Yes."

My heart sank into my stomach.

"Isn't your dad dead?"

"It is how we know if one of us can't talk."

"Call Captain and tell him we are on our way there."

It's about 45 minutes from Charleston to Beaufort. I make it in record time. I don't wait for backup. I draw my weapon and bust through the door, expecting to find my mom and the people who took Elizabeth.

"Clear," I yell to Taylor, who is a beat behind me.

"What did they do?"

"Asked me what you knew about the case and considering I didn't even know this was your case, they flew out of here."

"You got lucky, mom, but they took Elizabeth."

"The Captain called. He said take her to a safe house."

"I don't know what you got into, Sadie, but I do not like this at all." My mother says.

"I know."

I don't know how all of this is connected. I will find out, my mother doesn't know anything about this case or my dad's murder. It has to be connected to my dad's death at this point.

9

We take my mom to a safe house, so she is far away from this case. Now, we have to find Elizabeth or wire to funds.

It's been hours and the uni's have come up with nothing. It's like she vanished without a trace. McTeer hired some good criminals for this job. In and out, with no witnesses or evidence.

"Taylor and Johnson, go home. I will call you if we need anything."

"Still want to go back to my place?"

"It's better than mine."

We take my car since Taylor keeps extra clothes in his car. The ride home is quiet. A little too quiet.

"Do you think we will be safe?" He asked.

"I would like to think so, but at this point, probably not."

For the first time, I see real fear in his eyes. I search for the words comfort from him.

"At least I live on the 3rd floor."

"I know. That makes it safer than my apartment on ground level with lots of windows."

I nod in agreement. I wouldn't stay there either if I were him. We walk into the building, making sure the door shuts behind us, not letting anyone else enter that might be hiding in the shadows. We reach the third floor and I open my apartment. Stitches greeting us instantly.

"Sorry, he really is a needy cat since I rescued him."

"I never pictured you as a cat lady before."

I chucked because honestly I love all animals.

"I can make dinner," Taylor offers, opening up the pantry.

"Ok, I am going to go shower."

Normally I would leave my weapon by the door on the table, but tonight, I feel safer with it being with me. I listen for any unusual noises outside while taking a quick shower. I get dressed in my pajamas.

"It smells amazing."

"It's taco soup."

We sit at the bar, eating quietly. The fear is still strong on his face. He has barely even said much, considering he usually doesn't stop talking.

"Are you ok?" I asked quietly.

"Yeah, I just keep thinking we are next. Ya know?"

"Yeah, but at least we are together, so if anything does happen, hopefully it's two against one."

After we finish eating, I grab his blankets and a pillow from the closet. I keep double checking all the rooms in my apartment.

"I am just down the hall. Come get me if you hear anything suspicious."

He nods in agreement.

I climb into bed, listening to the surrounding quietness. I peer out the window down to the alley below. It's a calm night down there. Usually it is full of cats and car horns blaring at the traffic.

"Sadie.. Are you awake?"

"Yeah, what's wrong?" I said, turning on the lamp.

"I can't sleep."

"Me either."

Suddenly the power goes out. I peek out the window again. There is no storm, so someone must have cut the power. We hear the front door open and stitches hissing and running.

My eyes go wide.

"Where is your weapon?"

"With me."

"Get ready to use it."

We get on opposite sides of the door to my room. Waiting for someone to enter. Kane's eyes lock on mine, ready to shoot. The door opens and I take my stance. I feel hands grab around my wrist and pull me down. I stumble to get back up with I hear Kane and the other guy fighting. I grab my weapon off the ground and shoot. I take down the guy.

I run over to Kane, who is still on the ground under the guy. I lift him up, trying not to tamper with the evidence. Kane slides out from under him.

"Are you ok?"

"I wasn't hit, if that is what you are asking."

"We gotta call this in."

I rush to my side table to grab my phone to call it in when I get a text from an unknown number.

You won't be so lucky next time.

I roll my eyes at the screen. I am more determined to find the people responsible for attempted murder, kidnapping, and actual murder. All signs are pointing to McTeer.

The Captain shows up with a team.

EMT's check us out and gave me Tylenol. When I fell I landed on my wrist, which is now sore and throbbing.

"You guys got lucky tonight."

"I know. If it wasn't for Taylor being here, I might not be so lucky." I smile towards Kane and he tips his head in acknowledgement.

"We have to find who is responsible for all of this!"

"So, can we finally go undercover and get Kyle?"

"Fine, but thread lightly."

I will risk my career taking this man down. It seems like everyone forgot not long ago this man killed his own son. And yet everyone thinks he is innocent. Attacking my family is crossing the line. I will stop at nothing to prove he is guilty.

"Did we get Elizabeth back?"

I hear a deep sigh as he finds his words. "Her body was delivered."

It feels like a thousand bricks just fell onto of me. I blink my eyes, trying to press all of this is real. I feel Kane pull me in for a hug.

"We will find them together."

"Hey Captain, am I off the case for this or not?"

"No, it was justified."

At least I have that going for me. I watch as officers take evidence and photos. I observe them and how they are acting towards being in my apartment for a crime scene.

"I will make sure we have this cleaned up before you come back home tonight."

I nod in agreement. I really did not want to be cleaning up all this blood.

First thing tomorrow we are going back over all the bodies that seem to drop around McTeer.

"Want to start looking into connections now or when we go back to work?"

"Now." I say a little to sharply.

I huff and puff while I grab my laptop from the living room. I roll my eyes at the thought my apartment is a crime scene. I really thought we would be safe here, but it doesn't surprise me at all.

"Kane, you look into McTeer while I look at his son."

I start to google his son, a lot of social media presence. I need to see if he is connected in any way. I find news articles from when his mom died. He was also there when the maid died. I rub my face in frustration.

"His son has been at all the accidents that lead to death as well."

"Can't we use them against each other? See who cracks first?"

"I doubt that will work. They are intelligent, calculated, they will see that coming. We need actual evidence."

10

Today is the day we are bringing in McTeer's son, Nathan. I am nervous he will instantly know what we are up to. I slam my coffee back before Nathan arrives to be questioned.

I see them escorting the son to an interrogation room.

"I hope the son hasn't learned from his dad."

I side eye Taylor as we start to walk towards interrogation. I decided Taylor is going to lead him straight to the answers we desperately need.

"So tell me, how do so many accidents lead to dead bodies."

"The maid fell down."

"And died?"

"Yes. She hit her head on the steps and it cracked her skull."

"And your mother?"

"Slipped in the shower."

"Right. So how did she die?"

"I'm not really sure."

I nod to Taylor. I know he's just getting started, so I wait patiently.

"And tell me about Damon."

His face goes ghost white.

"Do you need water?" I asked.

"Please."

I hand him a cup of water while staring him down.

I sit next to Taylor.

"So, you do know Damon?"

"Yes…"

"What can you tell us?" I glance at look at Taylor, smiling like he has the perfect question.

"Was he in your dad's house when you burned it down?"

Still refusing to speak.

"Would you like a lawyer?"

"I think so."

We let him go and lucky for us he left his glass of water. I wait for him to leave the building.

"I am taking this straight to forensics."

Taylor walk beside me, "I think we scared him enough to warn his dad."

"That was the plan."

I am so happy the Captain agreed to tap his phone so we will now know everything. We finally make it to forensics.

"We need a rush on this."

"Ok I can probably have it in a few hours."

I give them a smile and we leave. Our forensic team quickly working on the DNA and will hopefully match something.

"My guess is McTeer forced his son to help."

"No, they aren't ones to get their hands dirty."

I hear my phone ding. I start walking as fast as possible. I grin at Taylor.

"He's texting right now with his dad."

We sit at my computer reading everything. So far, no one has admitted anything. They do have plans to meet tonight at the same wear house. Taylor's phone starts buzzing.

"I just got a text to meet at the same place."

"Agree and I will be there waiting."

This is perfectly falling into our hands. Now we just have to wait to see what they ask of Taylor before we move. We need to get everything recorded as evidence. Taylor already told the Captain about the money he received from McTeer to lead the cops away. Now we need to tell him that the undercover is going down tonight. After the attack in my apartment, Captain has been more than agreeing that I am right. All evidence leads straight to McTeer as the ringleader.

Now we just wait a few more hours.

I give Taylor his ear piece. "Are you ready?"

"No, I am a little nervous. They tried to take me out, too."

"I will be able to hear everything and I will be close by."

I watch him get into his car. I make sure to keep a distance between us in case anyone is following us.

"Sadie, can you hear me?"

"Yes."

"This has some distance to it."

"Yes, so it is recording, so once you go in, remember that."

I sit in a parking lot close by. I can hear everything going on.

"We need you to plant evidence to show it wasn't us."

"That broke into my partner's apartment and went to visit her mom?"

"And murder of Damon."

"What about Elizabeth?"

"I didn't order her to be murdered. I just wanted to use her to get some information."

"Anyone you want this pined on?"

"I don't care. Just do it."

"What is my payment?"

"We don't kill Sadie."

"Deal."

I intake a sharp gasp listening to this. It makes me more angry that they would use me as collateral. I must have been shocked by the news since I hear Kane in the ear piece asking if I recorded all of this.

"Hey Kane?"

"Meet me back at the station. I'm calling Captain to listen to this."

To my surprise, the Captain was still at work. We give the tape for him to listen.

"Well, Johnson, I guess you have everything you need."

"I told you I was right. I was going to be the one to arrest him."

"You can't and neither can Taylor. I want you both to stay alive."

We exchanged glances. "So who will do it?"

The Captain smiles proudly. "I will be the one."

Taylor and I pace around the station, waiting to hear anything. I know at this time, finding a judge to give us a search warrant is nearly impossible. The DA would ignore us to at this hour. I don't want to wait for morning. I also know with the deal Taylor took, I am safe for now. I still don't feel sad enough to go home.

I stay at the station all night. I have everything I need here. The coffee isn't that bad either. I know at my apartment, I wouldn't sleep. Kane is asleep at his desk. I eye him in jealously that he can sleep at a time like this.

"Did you two stay here all night?"

Rubbing my eyes, I try to gain focus. "It is the safest place in town."

"I didn't want to leave Sadie by herself in case."

I have the warrant for McTeer. I am waiting until I know he is at the law firm before I go get him.

I stumble to the break room to make coffee. I know it is going to be a long day with little sleep and no caffeine. While I wait for the coffee to make, I go to wash my face. The cold water splashing on my face wakes me up a little more.

"I have been waiting for you."

"What's up?"

"The captain went to get Mcteer."

That is news I wasn't expecting already.

"Captain didn't want to wait in case McTeer heard about the arrest warrant."

I nod.

I can't believe this is almost over. I am about to potentially get more information about my dad and Elizabeth. They didn't deserve to be murdered. They were good people. I take a pause before thinking about what happens next.

11

We wait for the word that the Captain arrested McTeer. Somehow, I don't feel like this is over. I can hear Taylor breathing loudly.

"Taylor, you're breathing so loudly."

"I am just breathing."

I get the word Captain is on the way with McTeer and he's already requested a lawyer. If only his son were so smart.

"I got a text from forensics saying they have something."

"Do you want me to go with?"

"Sure."

The walk to the elevator seems like an eternity. Taylor seems to be on edge. We finally reach the forensics.

"We have a match for the arson and murder of Damon."

My eyes grow wide, knowing it will be Kyle McTeer.

"Well, don't keep us waiting."

"Drum rolls please."

I shoot him a look.

"Alright, not in the mood, I see. It was McTeer's son."

"Nathan?"

"No. Landon."

"That explains so much."

"Did you find fingerprints on the weapon that killed my

dad?"

"Yes, that was Kyle McTeer."

I saw that coming. He was the officer on the scene when Amanda McTeer was murdered.

"Can you look into the other murders and see if the DNA matches?"

"Yeah, but that might take sometime. I would like to go shower."

"Fair enough."

I need to be sure the results are correct. I stand there looking at the computer screen.

"Are we sure they have not tampered the DNA?"

"I mean technically yeah, someone could place those prints on the bullets and trigger."

"Well, they are bringing Kyle in so he will lawyer up or confess. I bet he will lawyer up quick."

I call my mom since she is still in the safe house and give her an update that McTeer is arrested. She doesn't sound thrilled that she might be able to go home soon. I don't blame her. I haven't been back at my apartment since that night. I have been staying on Kane's couch. Once this case is solved, I can't wait to actually sleep in my bed. Stitches don't seem to mind staying at Kane's, since his windows are bigger than ours.

"Sadie, you ready to go watch the interrogation?"

"Yeah, we need to tell the Captain the DNA matched to Landon and Kyle."

After we get off the elevator, I catch a glimpse of McTeer smiling at Kane and me. My heart felt like it stopped at the moment. I can't begin to explain the evil look in that mans face. He knows Kane was helping us and now I feel like there is a target on both of us. My heart is pounding so loudly I can feel it in my ears. It's the worst feeling ever.

We watch from behind the glass and the Captain

interrogates McTeer. Something still feels off. Kane nudges me, pointing to the door. Legal counsel for McTeer has arrived. He is smart and calculated enough to know not to answer anything that could admit to guilt. We have nothing on McTeer to actually hold him, since the evidence points to his son. His wife's murder and the housekeeper could also be blamed on the son since he was there when it happened. Would McTeer let him take the fall?

I huff a little loud. Cases like this make me hate the legal system. Not enough evidence and all circumstantial when it comes to McTeer.

Taylor and I watch the interrogation from behind the glass. McTeer's body language suggests he's lying.

"McTeer is lying. Do you see how he keeps crossing his arms and looking away?"

"Yeah, I noticed that too."

Taylor leans in closer to the glass. "It looks like he's using his fingers to count."

"Count for what?"

"I'm not sure, but we need to talk to Nathan again. And like now."

I know we should go to talk to Nathan. I need to see how the interrogation goes. I know my mom is ready to go home. I am not convinced Landon killed anyone. I do think he has something to do with something at this point. The closer we get to an arrest, the more evidence is pushing in another direction.

"Taylor, did we ever check to see if they had another house keeper or nanny or someone that works for them?"

"Other than at the law office, no."

"We need to find out if anyone does or has in the past."

"Alright, but how?"

"I am exhausted to even know how to find the answers right now."

"We can regroup for tomorrow?" Taylor suggests.

"Yeah."

My apartment is finally no longer a crime scene. I know Kane didn't mind stitches and I being at his; I was ready to go home. I know Stitches miss his sunbathing in the window. I grab my keys from my desk, log off my computer, and head out for the night. Taylor and I walk to our cars.

"Do you think anything we learned in the interrogation is real?"

"I think some of it is real and I think some of it is lies to protect someone."

"You still think the son?"

"I do. Someone broke into my apartment, they attacked us both. It is safe to assume more will come. It's just about when and where."

"So, do you think my apartment is safe?"

"Honestly, Kane, probably not until we solve this case."

I hear him sigh. I know it's not what he wanted to hear, but it is the truth. I don't want to lie to my partner. I refuse to lie to him.

I get in my car and turn it on. I wait until Kane backs out of the parking space before I leave. The last thing I need is someone tampering with our cars. I couldn't be able to handle investigating another death that is close to me. We still don't know exactly what is going on with Elizabeth. It has my mother terrified I am getting too close. After my dad died on the force, she made me promise to never get too close to where I would be in danger like that. I feel like the suspicion of the McTeer's is getting too close. I need forensics to give me more. I need information on fibers, fingerprints, ballistics.

Tomorrow, we can are going to look at this case with all the angles on the board. The Captain and Kane are going to be so irritated. I am convinced we have the wrong person.

We arrive at Kane's. I grab Stitches and look around the

apartment.

"I think I have everything. If you find anything, just bring it to work."

"Wouldn't people think that is weird?"

"My apartment was a crime scene. My mother is in wit sec. I had nowhere else to go, so no."

"Does everyone know about your dad?"

Well, straight to the point.

"Yes. I just graduated from the academy when it happened. We don't get too many new recruits."

"Is that why you're such a by the book cop?"

"I take risk, I question things most people wouldn't think twice about. I have a Master's in forensics anthropology."

"And you are a cop?"

"It is a very competitive field, and I did not want a Ph.D."

"Interesting."

"I know we are still new at being partners. You will get the hang of it."

"I hope so."

I tell him bye and leave for my apartment with Stitches.

The drive home is quiet and hardly any traffic. I am happy about that. Tourist season can make the drive home unbearable.

I enter my apartment. It was cleaned before I came here. I peek into my bedroom, expecting to still see blood in the carpet. The cleaning team is good. Not a single drop spotted. I change out of my uniform and decide to take a shower in the morning. I am exhausted. Every limb feels like a thousand pounds. Stitches is curled up next to me, already sleeping. I hear little purrs escaping from him. I wish I could fall asleep as easily as him.

12

Morning comes so early. I don't even feel like I slept at all. Stitches is already meowing for his breakfast. I fix his food before taking a quick shower. I make a large pot of coffee. While I wait for it to finish, I start taking notes to show Taylor when we get to work. I grab more note cards, writing all the facts down. Next, I write all the evidence down. Lastly, I write everything else that has happened that so far is a dead end or at least unexplainable. I hear the coffee maker beep, signaling it is done. I fill my thermos full. I pet Stitches bye before I walk out the door.

I pull into the parking lot and park next to Taylor. I am surprised he beat me here. I am usually the first. I walk inside looking for him.

"Hey," I hear from behind me.

"I was looking for you. It surprised me you beat me here."

"I couldn't sleep."

"I don't think I slept much either."

"I bet Stitches did," Taylor says as he chuckles.

"Always."

He follows me to my desk. "I have note cards on the case. I have them into 3 categories. 1st category is facts, second is crimes and third is everything that is a dead end or still investigating."

"You think this will help?"

"It will help to regain focus and maybe see what we are missing."

"I think we are missing something. Either a connection or a person."

I lay out the facts and crimes note cards on my desk, starting with the explosion and dead body. I still can't see any connection other than Kyle McTeer.

"Do you have any sting?"

"Maybe in my desk."

I search for sting on my desk. I open the case file that we have so far, making sure they aren't missing anything.

"So Nathan's fingerprints are on the bullets and trigger from my dad's murder. Landon's was on the bullet we found at the house. So what about the housekeeper and Amanda McTeer?"

"Still no update. Lack of evidence."

"There has to be something. I do not believe the sons actually did it. I almost feel like they were placed there."

"We still don't know who sent the weapon to you."

I see Taylor shift his weight to one leg. "You think it was your sister?"

"Only one way to know for sure."

" I will bring her in. I don't want you there in case the McTeers find out."

I call up Taylor's sister, Mckenzy Taylor. I tell her I need her to come to the station and didn't leave much room to tell her why.

While I wait for her, I call my mother to see how she is doing. I am happy she is still at the safe house. Even though I told her it was probably safe to go home; she did not feel like it was. Honestly, I wouldn't go home either after someone killed Elizabeth and took her.

"Are you officer Johnson?"

"You must be McKenzie."

"How can you tell?"

"I work with your brother. You guys look alike. Always follow me."

I take her to the interrogation room. She sits down and I sit across from her.

"Did you leave a package for me on the steps of the station?"

Her face freezes and she crosses her arms.

"I did. I knew it was Landon's, and I saw Kyle McTeer peaking around my apartment. I think he was looking for it. I didn't know what to do. I knew your name from my bother talking about you. I knew you would know what to do."

"Are you aware of the crimes this weapon was used for?"

"No, I didn't even know they fired it. I just knew if Kyle was in my apartment, it must be bad."

"How do you know Kyle was in your apartment?"

"I have hidden cameras. I don't trust people and I live alone, so if anyone breaks in, I wanted to have proof."

"Can I see the film?"

"Yeah, I have it stored on my phone."

I take her phone and save the recording.

"One last question. Are you scared of the McTeer's?"

"I mean, I never saw anything. I just know after Amanda died, the family kind of fell apart. I don't think the boys had anything to do with it."

"Ok, well, don't leave town. If we need to question you again, I will."

She walks out of the room, leading her on the way to the front doors. Just when I thought this case was solved. We had evidence, Kyle's half confession. And now I have more reasonable doubt about who is the mastermind behind the whole thing.

"How was my sister?"

"She was very helpful. She was the one that sent me the package."

"I wonder if Landon left it at her apartment?"

"Me too, and why Kyle would think so? Check hers."

"Something seems weird."

I agree something is weird. Right now, McKenzie isn't a suspect. She wasn't even on the radar until the gun was delivered to me. If it wasn't for Kane, I never would have thought the ex-girlfriend would have anything to do with it. Mckenzy Taylor doesn't seem like a person that could murder a man or set fire to a house. I told her not to leave town in case we need to ask more questions, but right now she is not a suspect.

I carefully analyze the film McKenzie gave me. Kyle seems to move cool and confident through her apartment like he has been there. I notice he knows exactly where the closets are and searching through all of time. Kyle rips through her clothes before leaving. He leaves empty-handed. Whatever he is looking for, he can't find. Which if it was the weapon, then it would make sense because it was already in our possession. If this video was three days ago, why would Kyle think of searching her apartment, anyway? I can't think of any logical explanation.

"Does McKenzie still have contact with any of the McTeers?"

"I don't think so. But I have never really asked her to be honest. I assumed once they broke up, she cut ties, since she said Landon went a little crazy after his mom."

"Do you believe her?"

"I don't have any reason not to yet and neither do you," he says, shifting his weight again.

"I am more focused on the McTeer's and motive, means and opportunity. I believe the dad is the behind the planning and the sons are doing the crimes. I just have to connect all the crimes back to Kyle. And I keep coming up short with evidence to connect all the crimes."

"We could charge them for separate crimes and then see who will be the first to break."

"Possible."

While I know Kyle was behind the break in at my apartment. The body downstairs doesn't have any person's artifacts with them. I am still waiting on a positive ID of who that person is. Once we find out the name, we will hopefully find a connection to one of the McTeers. I can't wait for this to be over. I look at the time.

"I think I am going to head out. Want to go grab a drink?" I asked Taylor.

"Yeah. I do. Today was rough."

Kane follows me to the local bar. I decided to sit on the rooftop. It is a nice, cool night. We pick a table that overlooks the ocean.

"I love how peaceful the beach looks from here."

'The beach is peaceful, Kane. Waves crashing on top of you, the sand rushing back into the water. The whole experience of the ocean is relaxing and peaceful."

"I hate how sand gets everywhere."

"Baby powder on your skin will make the sand brush off easy."

I listen to him order his drink and I order mine. I sit in silence, listening to the waves lap onto the shore.

"You know, I thought I would feel better being this close to finding out the truth, but the more I learn, the more I don't want to think about how they became this way."

"I get it. I just hope my sister isn't involved."

"I hope so too, and so far, it does seem that way. We don't have anything on her or to even think she is involved."

I watch him take another sip, "if it we do find out she is

involved, what do you want to do?"

"I want you to be the one that will arrest her."

"I promise I will. I will make sure we do everything right."

"I trust you, Sadie.I think of you as a friend and my partner."

The waitress bring us our bill. Kane pays for it this time. I have to go home to Stitches. I know he is curled up in my chair, waiting for me to get home.

I drive home from the beach. I wish I could afford an apartment closer to the beach. With my salary, I would need a roommate to afford it. I love Sam. I couldn't live with her. She is too messy even for me. She also works too late and so do I. One day, I will find an apartment at the beach. The drive isn't bad. It only takes about 20 minutes to get to the beach. Even with traffic, that maybe adds about 10 minutes and that is usually to just find parking.

I enter my apartment, Stitches is curled in my chair sleeping. I pour his food into his bowl, making him perk up. I make my way to the shower. I need to wash off the day. It will make the stress melt away.

Thinking about this case and the murders, I know I have to question McKenzie more. I need to know if there is still a connection. I log onto social media searching for Mckenzie. She is still friend with Landon on social media. I search her friends to see if I see Nathan on the list. Next I will find if she is friends with Amanda or Kyle. I doubt she is, but it is still worth checking out. It will at least tell me if I need to question her about the McTeer's again. The water starts turning cold. I turn off the water and change into my pajamas. The one thing I dislike about being a cop is the fact it is hard to see the good in people anymore. There is so much evil in the world that yo can't trust anyone.

I turn on the TV to see if the news is talking about this case. Our department isn't speaking with the media yet, but it is only a matter of time before they hear about this. I flip through the local channels, scanning for anything. I see McKenzie on the news, speaking about her part in being questioned. I should have told her not to speak to anyone about this. Now she has a target on her. I hear my phone ringing.

"Hey Kane." I answer.

"Mckenzie is on the news talking about being questioned by the cops."

"I am watching it right now. Why is she doing this?"

"I don't know and now everyone is going to know the McTeer's are the suspects in the fire and multiple murders."

"I don't know what to do about it."

"Come over, we can figure it out."

I just wanted the day to be over, not wanting to deal with McKenzie talking to the media about her questioning over McTeer. And now everyone knows what is going on. I hope they don't put a target on her. I finish watching the segment while waiting for Kane to arrive.

I hear him knocking. I pad over to let him in.

"It got worse, Kane."

"She said they wrongfully questioned her about a package she didn't deliver. She told us she sent it to me because she didn't want you involved and didn't know what to do with it."

"This doesn't sound like Mckenzie. I am starting to think Landon is holding something over her."

"Kyle already tried to get you to tamper with evidence."

"I should probably talk to the Captain about this and find out our next steps."

"Yes, but we need you on this case because of the money, and Kyle thinks you will help him."

"Sadie, this is already so messed up and dangerous. How much worse could it actually get?"

"Do you want me to answer?"

"Yeah."

"Murder one of us. And my guess it will be you."

"That is worst. Why did you want me to come over?"

"If they are smart, they probably have our phones bugged."

"What about your apartment?"

"No, after the break in I check once I get home. It's clear."

I wait for the silence to pass. The panic is clear on Kane's face.

"We could go see McKenzie. It is only 8."

"I'll drive."

Kane stands to walk to the door. I grab my keys and lock the door behind us. The walk to his car is silent. He turns on the car and backs out of the parking space.

"It's only been 10 days. It is going to take some time to find answers to how complex this case is getting. Just be grateful we have some answers already. Something like this could literally take months to figure out."

He nods in my direction as we pull up to her apartment building. It is a house that was transformed into apartments.

"She is in 3C."

I will follow you. We head up the stairs. Kane stops in front of her door, listening for movement and sounds.

"I hear voices," he mouthed.

I lean my ear closer to the door. I hear faint voices. One sounds like McKenzie and I can't make out the other voice. We hear glass breaking. Kane kicks in the door. McKenzie is standing over Nathan.

I rush to Nathan, checking for a pulse and injuries. I hear him start to mumble. I can't make out what he said. Kane is calling 911.

"He has cuts on his forehead."

Kane starts to question her while Nathan is trying to sit up.

"I didn't do it."

"You are the only person here, McKenzie. So what happened?"

"I heard a knock, and I opened the door. Nathan rushed in, looking for Landon. I told him I didn't know where he was. He started getting angry, and I felt threatened, so I hit him with the vase."

"Lawyer," said Nathan.

I watch over his shoulder as he text his dad he needs a lawyer and will explain later.

"Kane, you have to believe me."

"It's Officer Taylor, and no, I don't have to believe anything other than the facts. I don't see signs of a struggle or anything."

Taylor reads Mckenzie her Miranda rights and handcuffs here.

EMT's arrival checking out Nathan. They give him medicine and bandage his head.

The other officers take McKenzie and we take Nathan back to the station. So much for having a relaxing night.

Once at the station, we interrogate Mckenzie.

"I could never murder anyone."

"You hit Nathan with a vase."

"It is not murder. He will be fine."

I run my hands over my face. While yes, he is fine, it could be much worst.

"The best thing you can do right now is tell us everything you know," I tell her.

McKenzie adjusts in her chair.

"Nathan came to me looking for Landon. I have told you this."

"No, I want to know why Kyle was in your apartment and how does he know where you live?"

"I've had this apartment since I was in college. It's not hard to figure that out. Landon was always here, so I am sure that is how Kyle knows."

"And what's your relationship with Landon now?"

"Nothing. We don't even talk."

I gather the file. Taylor walks out first. I follow behind him. We go to the other side of the glass, observing her. McKenzie starts fiddling with her fingers and twirling her hair.

"She is hiding something."

"Yep, now we have to find out what."

13

Interrogation with McKenzie didn't go as expected. Kane thought she would confess her part in the whole crime. Now it is time to shift the focus from McKenzie and Landon. I know this will be hard for Kane to think his sister has a part in murders. I also know he wants to help me find the truth. Solving innocent people's murder is more important than protecting his sister. What is stopping her from killing other innocent people? Two families are going to be ripped apart.

"Johnson. My office now."

"Yes?"

"You, along with Officer Taylor, think his sister McKenzie is covering for the McTeer's?"

"I don't think it's a bad idea to investigate since she assaulted Nathan McTeer in her apartment last night."

"I see. Is Taylor too close to this?"

"No, I am almost positive he wants to find the answers, just like I do."

"Make sure it stays that way."

I nod towards the Captain , turning on my heels to leave.

Walking as fast as I can, I sit at my desk with my hands cupping my face. How did we even get here? There has to be something I am missing. I am tired of looking at this case from the beginning every time something irrational happens. I need to find a connecting factor of why are these crimes are happening. Whatever the reason, they all have a connection and, so far, no motive for any of them.

What's the motive for Kyle shooting Damon? What's the motive for his wife? And the motive for the housekeeper?

The only one that makes sense is the arson. He had to burn his house down to cover the tracks of the murder and destroy all evidence with it. Could McKenzie's voice be the scream Elizabeth heard before the gunshot? I grab the recording of the 911 call. I don't hear anything from inside the home except the scream and gun shot. I need to hear McKenzie scream. I need something to tell us why if she was at the house.

My phone starts ringing, breaking me from my thought.

"Hello?"

"I got something you want to see. And grab Taylor."

"Be right there."

I grab Taylor while heading for the elevator. He passes me a coffee while I hit the first floor.

"Forensics said we need to see something."

He nods as he steps out of the elevator.

"Guys. We have finally pieced together McTeer's book that was found at the fire."

Taylor looks at me, "Well?"

"We see McKenzie's name and how much he paid her. We do not see why."

"What about Landon and Nathan?"

"There names are there too."

With wide eyes, Taylor turns to me, "We have to get to McKenzie before the McTeers do."

We didn't have enough to hold her in custody. I think we finally have enough now. With this new information, she has to tell us.

"While we are out, we need to check on Nathan."

"Alright."

"Do you want to be there when your sister is arrested? I understand if you don't."

"Yes, if she had anything to do with all of this, I need to know why."

I walk with Taylor back to my desk to grab my keys. I grab them and motion for him to go to my car. I can't imagine how he must feel about his sister at this moment. She went from being a person of interest to someone we think was the mastermind behind the whole plan.

The drive to her apartment is quiet. It doesn't feel right. I know I can't just go on with my gut feelings, but there has to be something we missed. Or at least something we don't know yet. Taylor's expression seems a little too anxious about the situation.

We get to her apartment. I really don't like the feeling of this. I walk in front of Taylor. I wait until he catches up. I knock on her door.

"Who is it?"

I nod at Kane.

"It's me. Let me in."

I hear her pacing around before walking to the door.

"Oh, no."

"We just want to talk."

I walk in, letting Kane do all the talking.

"We need to know what is going on."

She motions to the lap. My eyes go wide as I pull out my notebook. I write out did there a bug in here? She nods to me. I know we have to make it seem like its just her brother here. I tell them to just talk.

"Let's go get dinner. I've missed spending time with you," Kane says.

McKenzie walks out of her apartment. I motion for them to

follow me. We arrive at my car and we get inside.

"Who bugged your apartment?"

"McTeer."

"Why?"

"Well, I made the comments to the news and he is getting scared I will start talking. You have to believe me. McTeer is setting me up."

"The evidence is piling high against you."

"I will prove I am innocent."

"How?"

She pulls out her phone. There are emails from an unknown address demanding she not talk to the police. More emails about money.

"This is pretty evident that someone is setting you up. But we need to print these and send them to our forensics teams."

"Anything to clear my name."

I take her to my apartment where I sent the emails to the forensics team. I call them and demand it be a rush job. I print out the emails on my printer.

If McKenzie wasn't innocent, she wouldn't have these emails. This is telling me McTeer is the mastermind and wanted us to think she was responsible.

"Does anyone know that you have evidence?"

"We have kept it pretty tight. It is on a need to know bases around here."

"I want you to either stay with me or with Kane tonight until we can figure out what to do next."

She agrees to stay with me. My apartment was already attacked, so I figured mine would be safer than Kane's. McTeer could just show up since Kane is supposed to be telling him what is going on with the case and destroying evidence.

I sit and think while I listen to Kane and McKenzie talk. The noise is helping me focus on finding what is actually happening. I stopped my thoughts when Kane's phone rings. I lean in closer to hear what is being said. Motioning him to put it on speaker, he does. I am taken aback by the demands.

"Clean up the mess your sister made or I will show all the evidence she is guilty of murder."

McKenzie's face drops, holding her face. There has to be a reason they want to blame Mckenzie.

"We have to figure this out here. At the apartment."

I pull out index cards and pens for everyone. McKenzie put the timeline together of her relationship with the McTeers. I put together the evidence in order we have found. Kane writes about his involvement with Mcteer.

"Hello?"

"We got a search warrant. We finally go McTeer."

"Do you need us to come in?"

"Yes."

"Be there in 20."

I hang up with the Captain . I grab Kane and tell McKenzie to stay at my apartment and don't let anyone in.

We rush to the station. Captain is already in the interrogation room with McTeer and his lawyer. I listen to all the answers. He doesn't admit to anything. He also doesn't take a plea. It is finally over. I watch as they hand cuff him and take him away. It is fine since we have all the evidence that he murdered my dad, his wife and the housekeeper. Landon doesn't have any evidence against him nor does Nathan. They are guilty of something but not murder.

"I can't believe it is over."

"Me either," I tell Kane.

www.ingramcontent.com/pod-product-compliance
Lightning Source LLC
Chambersburg PA
CBHW040912010826